S0-DOR-420

The 12 Days of Lunar New Year

by Jenna Lettice • illustrated by Colleen Madden

A Random House PICTUREBACK® Book

Random House New York

rhcbooks.com
Library of Congress Control Number: 2020020704
ISBN 978-0-593-30678-9 (trade) — ISBN 978-0-593-30679-6 (ebook)
MANUFACTURED IN CHINA 10 9 8 7 6 5 4 3 2

On the **first** day
of Lunar New Year,
my parents gave to me:

One dancing dragon
for luck.

On the **second** day of Lunar New Year, my parents gave to me:

Two sweet rice cakes and one dancing dragon for luck.

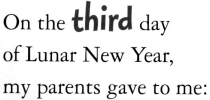

On the **third** day
of Lunar New Year,
my parents gave to me:

Three brave lions,
Two sweet rice cakes,
and one dancing dragon
for luck.

On the **fourth** day of
Lunar New Year,
my parents gave to me:

Four red envelopes,
Three brave lions,
Two sweet rice cakes,
and one dancing dragon
for luck.

On the **fifth** day
of Lunar New Year,
my parents gave to me:

Five tangerines!

Four red envelopes,
Three brave lions,
Two sweet rice cakes,
and one dancing dragon
for luck.

On the **sixth** day
of Lunar New Year,
my parents gave to me:

Six brooms for sweeping,
Five tangerines!
Four red envelopes,
Three brave lions,
Two sweet rice cakes,
and one dancing dragon
for luck.

On the **seventh** day
of Lunar New Year,
my parents gave to me:

Seven friends to shop with,
Six brooms for sweeping,
Five tangerines!
Four red envelopes,
Three brave lions,
Two sweet rice cakes,
and one dancing dragon
for luck.

On the **eighth** day
of Lunar New Year,
my parents gave to me:

Eight dumplings cooking,
Seven friends to shop with,
Six brooms for sweeping,
Five tangerines!
Four red envelopes,
Three brave lions,
Two sweet rice cakes,
and one dancing dragon
for luck.

On the **ninth** day
of Lunar New Year,
my parents gave to me:

Nine lanterns glowing,
Eight dumplings cooking,
Seven friends to shop with,
Six brooms for sweeping,
Five tangerines!
Four red envelopes,
Three brave lions,
Two sweet rice cakes,
and one dancing dragon
for luck.

On the **tenth** day
of Lunar New Year,
my parents gave to me:

Ten people feasting,
Nine lanterns glowing,
Eight dumplings cooking,
Seven friends to shop with,
Six brooms for sweeping,
Five tangerines!
Four red envelopes,
Three brave lions,
Two sweet rice cakes,
and one dancing dragon
for luck.

On the **eleventh** day
of Lunar New Year,
my parents gave to me:

Eleven fireworks,
Ten people feasting,
Nine lanterns glowing,
Eight dumplings cooking,
Seven friends to shop with,
Six brooms for sweeping,
Five tangerines!
Four red envelopes,
Three brave lions,
Two sweet rice cakes,
and one dancing dragon
for luck.

On the **twelfth** day
of Lunar New Year,
my parents gave to me:

Twelve zodiac animals,
Eleven fireworks,
Ten people feasting,
Nine lanterns glowing,
Eight dumplings cooking,
Seven friends to shop with,
Six brooms for sweeping,
Five tangerines!
Four red envelopes,
Three brave lions,
Two sweet rice cakes . . .

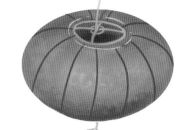

. . . and one dancing dragon for luck.

Happy New Year!

恭喜发财，新年好！